DISNEY's
First Year Book
2002

Disney's
First Year Book
2002

Published by Grolier Books

Grolier Books is a division of Grolier Enterprises, Inc.

FERN L. MAMBERG   *Executive Editor*

ELIZABETH A. DeBELLA   *Designer*

KAY SIEPIETOSKI   *Production Manager*

ISBN: 0-7172-1105-3
ISSN: 1098-5107

Stories on pages 6–17, 24–35, 42–53, 60–71, 78–89, and all Disney character illustrations copyright © 1998 by Disney Enterprises, Inc. Pages 90–91: Based on the *Pooh* stories by A. A. Milne, copyright © The Pooh Properties Trust.

PRINTED IN THE UNITED STATES OF AMERICA

Illustration Credits and Acknowledgments

18-19—© Art Wolfe; 19—© Lanz Von Horsten/A.B.P.L.; © Art Wolfe; © Animals Animals; 20—© Clem Haagner/Photo Researchers, Inc.; © Stephen J. Krasemann/DRK Photo; 20-21—© Art Wolfe; 21—© Tom & Pat Leeson; © Hans Reinhard/Bruce Coleman Inc.; 36—© Michael A. Keller/The Stock Market; 37—© Gary Meszaros/Bruce Coleman Inc.; © C.C. Lockwood/Animals Animals; 38—© J.C. Carton/Bruce Coleman Inc.; © Doug Wechsler/Animals Animals; 39—© Fred Bavendam; 54—© Berg Alistair-Spoon/Gamma Liaison; © Superstock; 55—Courtesy, Ringling Bros. and Barnum & Bailey Combined Shows; 56—© David Woods/The Stock Market; 57—Courtesy, Ringling Bros. and Barnum & Bailey Combined Shows; © Robert McElroy/Woodfin Camp & Associates; 58—Courtesy, Ringling Bros. and Barnum & Bailey Combined Shows; 59—© Tom Hanson/Gamma Liaison; 72—© Ron Kimball; 73—© Ariel Skelley/The Stock Market; © Ralph A. Reinhold/Animals Animals; © ZEFA Germany/The Stock Market; 74-75—© Richard Orr; 76—Tom & Deeann McCarthy/The Stock Market; 77—© J. Barry O'Rourke/The Stock Market; 92—© W. Gregory Brown/Animals Animals; 92-93—© Gregory Ochocki/Photo Researchers, Inc.; 93—© Neil G. McDaniel/Photo Researchers, Inc.; © Dale Kneupfer/Bruce Coleman Inc.; 94—© Jane Burton/Bruce Coleman Inc.; © Carl Roessler/Animals Animals; 94-95—© Gregory Ochocki/Photo Researchers, Inc.; 95—© Bill Wood/ Bruce Coleman Inc.; © Denise Tackett/Tom Stack & Associates

Contents

The Princess and the Jester

Once upon a time, a king, a queen, and a princess lived in a big castle in a beautiful valley. But a scary giant lived in a cave nearby.

One day, Princess Minnie decided to visit her very best friend, Princess Clarabelle, who lived in the next kingdom. The king's two bravest knights—Sir Donald and Sir Goofy—would go with Princess Minnie to keep her safe.

On the day before Princess Minnie's journey, the jester was doing tricks to amuse the royal family. "Your majesty, I, er, oops!" said Mickey, as he slipped on a banana peel. The king laughed. Next, Mickey made a bouquet of flowers magically appear. Everybody clapped.

Then Mickey shyly asked the king, "May I help keep Princess Minnie safe on her journey?"

"Ha, ha!" laughed the king. "*You*, Jester? How can *you* keep her safe?"

"Well, then, Sire, may I go along to keep Princess Minnie amused?" Mickey asked. The princess smiled at Mickey, and he was filled with joy. The jester was deeply in love with the princess.

"Minnie?" asked the king. "Do you wish it?"

"Oh, yes, Father!" said the princess. For she was secretly in love with Mickey.

The next day Princess Minnie, Sir Donald, Sir Goofy, and the jester set off. They kept very quiet when they passed the giant's cave. Luckily, he was fast asleep.

When the royal party got to the next kingdom,
Princess Clarabelle rushed out to meet them.
"Minnie!" exclaimed Princess Clarabelle. The two
princesses hugged each other. Then Princess
Clarabelle said to the two knights and the jester,
"Welcome, everyone! I hope you will all have a good
time in my kingdom."

Princess Clarabelle's lady-in-waiting, Lady Daisy, smiled at Sir Donald. Sir Donald kissed her hand, and off they went for a walk.

Sir Horace, Princess Clarabelle's bravest knight, whispered to Sir Goofy. "Come help me work on my new secret weapon."

Mickey stayed behind with the two princesses and entertained them.

Several days later it was time to leave. The two princesses sadly said good-bye. Lady Daisy asked Sir Donald to write to her. Sir Horace insisted that Sir Goofy take his secret weapon to show the king.

Unfortunately, when they reached the cave, the giant was awake and standing in the road.

Sir Donald bravely threw his spear at the giant. But the giant caught it and broke it in half.

"Time for Sir Horace's secret weapon," Sir Goofy said. The secret weapon was a giant slingshot. It

could send boulders flying through the air. But
instead of a boulder, Goofy accidentally sent *himself*
flying through the air. And the giant batted Goofy
aside as if he were a fly.

"Will we ever be able to get home?" sighed
Princess Minnie.

"Don't worry. We'll think of something," Mickey
answered.

They all sat down and tried to think of something
else to do. The giant sat down, too. Mickey rested
his chin on his fists. The giant rested his chin on his

fists. Mickey scratched his head. The giant scratched his head. Mickey whispered to Princess Minnie, "I have an idea. Wait here."

Mickey stood up. The giant stood up. Mickey shook his head from side to side. The giant shook his head from side to side. Mickey tiptoed in a circle

with his arms over his head like a ballerina. The giant did the same. Whatever Mickey did, the giant did too!

The game with the giant continued. Mickey hopped this way. The giant hopped this way. Mickey skipped that way. The giant skipped that way. Then Mickey hopped and skipped into the giant's cave. . .and the giant hopped and skipped right behind him. When Mickey and the giant were out of sight, the others hurried on and made their way home.

But where was Mickey? Days went by with no sign of him. Princess Minnie was so sad that she told her parents about her love for the jester.

The queen said, "The jester was very brave. If he returns, you and he may marry."

"Thank you, Mother," cried Princess Minnie.

Just then a booming sound was heard in the distance. Everyone rushed out onto the balcony. The booming grew louder and clearer: "Hiya! HIYA! Hellooo! HELLOOO!"

The royal family stared in disbelief as the happy giant appeared before them—with Mickey sitting on his shoulder.

The giant gently put Mickey down on the ground. Princess Minnie ran to him and sighed, "Oh, Mickey, I'm so glad you're safe!"

"Gee, Princess," sighed Mickey right back. "Will you. . .will you—" he started to ask.

"Yes, I will marry you!" cried Princess Minnie, before the jester could even finish asking his question.

Then the king commanded, "Kneel, Jester!"

"Y-y-yes, Your Majesty," Mickey said.

"For acts of bravery and tricks of magic, I dub thee Sir Mickey. Arise!" the king said.

"Oh, Mickey, I mean, *Sir* Mickey!" exclaimed Princess Minnie.

The joyful couple hugged each other and began to plan for their wedding. They would invite friends from every kingdom. And no one would be afraid to come, because never again would anybody be afraid of the jolly giant.

A big hug from Mom makes everything okay for a cuddly baby monkey. It isn't easy growing up in the wild! Animal parents work very hard to feed, clean, and protect their babies. They also teach their babies all the things they will need to know when they grow up. This baby monkey already knows to cling tightly to Mom—so he won't fall out of the tree!

Bringing Up Baby

Baby birds open their mouths wide for food. Their parents bring them tasty bugs, but the little birds are always hungry. "More! More!" they peep. The adults spend all day feeding their hungry chicks.

A baby bobcat looks like a fluffy kitten. Its spotted coat is just like its mother's. As this cub grows up, the mother bobcat will teach it how to hunt.

A lamb has found the perfect hiding place: Mom! This mother and baby are Dall sheep. They live high in the mountains. The woolly lamb will grow up to be a sure-footed mountain climber, just like its mother.

Some penguins are super parents. These birds live in icy Antarctica. It's cold! But the parents keep their chicks warm. They hold the chicks on their feet and cover them with their feathery bellies.

Baby meerkats have baby-sitters! These African animals live in big groups. And the whole clan helps raise the babies. If mothers go in search of food, others watch the kids.

An elephant baby stays close to Mom. It looks tiny next to her. But it's a really big baby! Elephant moms and "aunts"—other females—spend years teaching their babies elephant ways.

Bath time! An elk washes her calf with her tongue. The little calf has knobby knees and spindly legs. But a calf can stand and walk just hours after it is born.

Mom is a moving home for a baby kangaroo, or joey. A joey spends most of its first year in its mother's pouch, growing big and strong. By the time a joey is as big as this one, it's about ready to hop out of the pouch for good.

MAKE A PINECONE BIRD FEEDER

"Meeko," says Pocahontas, "stop eating that food. It's for the birds!"

Pocahontas loves to feed her feathered friends. Would you like to invite the birds in *your* neighborhood for a meal? Then make this pinecone bird feeder. Soon finches, sparrows, chickadees, and other birds will visit your backyard for a yummy snack.

What you need:

- pinecones
- a jar of peanut butter
- birdseed
- a piece of yarn
- a spoon
- newspaper to work on

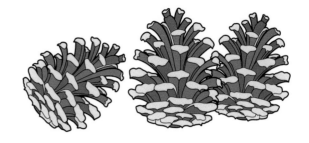

1. Gather a few pinecones. You might find some on a walk through the woods. Or you can buy them at a craft store.

2. With the spoon, spread peanut butter all over one pinecone. Make sure to stuff lots of it between the pinecone's scales. Then roll the pinecone in birdseed.

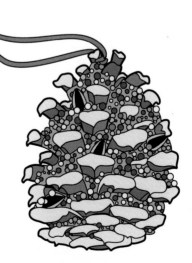

3. Tie a piece of yarn around the top of the pinecone. Ask an adult to hang the pinecone from a tree branch near a window of your house. Now just wait for the hungry birds to visit.

THE THUNDERBOLT SHOW

Thunderbolt raced across the television screen. He was being chased by Dirty Dawson.

"Run, Thunderbolt, run!" shouted Lucky as he and the other pups watched the TV show.

When the show was over, Perdita said to the pups, "Go outside and play now."

"But, Mother—" Lucky wanted to watch more television.

"Now, Lucky," Perdita said firmly.

Lucky went outside. But he was so bored. There just wasn't anything to do. Suddenly he spotted a large brown box. A big hole was torn out of the front of it. Patch was napping inside. To Lucky, the box looked just like a TV!

If I can't watch television, Lucky thought, maybe I can *play* it! Let's see now. . .Rolly can do the commercial, and Penny can be the announcer. And Patch can be Dirty Dawson, since he already has a black eye.

"Wake up, Patch!" Lucky said. "We're going to put on the Thunderbolt Show right here."

"What?" Patch yawned. "The Thunderbolt Show is coming here?" he repeated just as Rolly and Penny came over.

"Yep," answered Lucky. "And soon Thunderbolt himself will be here!" Since the game was his idea, Lucky decided that *he* would play Thunderbolt. He left to find a costume.

But the other puppies didn't quite understand. "Thunderbolt is coming here!" they cried. They wagged their tails and ran off to tell all their friends.

Soon Lucky came back to the box with a magazine picture he was going to use as a Thunderbolt mask. He was surprised to see that the backyard was full of hundreds of pups and dogs. They were yapping excitedly.

It took a minute before Lucky could make out their words. "Thunderbolt's coming!" "A real star in our own backyard!" "When will he be here, Lucky?" "Where's Thunderbolt?"

The dogs kept asking more and more questions. Lucky dropped the picture he was carrying. "Wait a minute," he said nervously. He ducked behind the box to try to come up with a plan. But what was he

going to do? Lucky wanted to run away. Then he thought, what would the real Thunderbolt do? Lucky realized that he would have to tell the truth. He went to face the crowd.

"I'm sorry, everyone," Lucky began. "I didn't mean to—" But before he could finish, he heard a loud bark and saw a car at the front of his house. And leaning out the window was the real Thunderbolt!

"Hello! Hello!" Thunderbolt barked. All the dogs raced over to him. Then Lucky's parents came out of the house.

Lucky heard his father say, "Well, hello, Thunderbolt. This is quite a surprise." Pongo looked around at the puppies and dogs. "I wonder how your fan club knew you would be here."

Thunderbolt said, "It's certainly a surprise to me. My crew and I were filming our television

show nearby. We were going home and lost our way. When I saw all the Dalmatians, I knew this must be the home of the famous Pongos. All of dogdom knows you."

Just then, Lucky became brave enough to talk to Thunderbolt. "Would you show us some of your tricks, Thunderbolt?"

Pongo smiled. "This is my son, Lucky. He's your biggest fan."

Thunderbolt bowed. "I would be delighted to perform." He turned to Lucky. "All right, son, you can be Dirty Dawson." Lucky yapped happily.

"Ready?" Thunderbolt called to Lucky. Then Thunderbolt raced across the backyard with Lucky

close behind. Without warning, Thunderbolt stopped, turned, and soared through the air—right over Lucky's head.

"That's my fast getaway," Thunderbolt said.

All the dogs barked their approval.

"I'm afraid it's time for me to go now," said
Thunderbolt. "It was wonderful meeting you all.
The next time we come here to film our show, you
must come to see me."

Pongo, Perdita, and all the Dalmatian puppies and
their friends barked and yapped their thanks to
Thunderbolt.

Everybody watched Thunderbolt climb into the car. Then he leaned out the window to give one final good-bye bark.

"He's quite a nice dog," Pongo said. "We were very lucky to meet him."

"Very lucky," Lucky agreed. He sighed with relief.

"And, Mother," said Lucky, "you were right about playing outside. It's better than watching TV!"

Perdita smiled as she watched Lucky trot over to the box.

I wonder how Lucky knew that Thunderbolt was coming, Patch thought. He went over to the box to ask. But he didn't get an answer.

Lucky was fast asleep, dreaming about his next adventure with Thunderbolt.

A WALK ON THE BEACH

Let's go for a walk on the beach! What will we find? The ocean carries all kinds of things to the shore and leaves them there. Shells, rocks, and many other treasures lie in the sand, waiting for you to spot them. Look closely as you walk along.

36

Seashells come in so many shapes and colors! There are fat spirals and long tubes. Some shells have two parts that are hinged together. Some are white or light gray. Some are brightly colored, with stripes or spots.

All the shells on the beach once belonged to snails and similar ocean animals. These animals made the shells and lived in them. The animals are gone, but they left their shells for you to find.

Go Shell Hunting

How many different shells can you find at the beach? Ask your parents to take you on a shell hunt. The best times to look for shells are at low tide and after a storm. Take a pail or a plastic bag to carry the shells you find. But if a shell has an animal inside, make sure to leave the shell behind.

This is a sand dollar—the dried skeleton of a little ocean animal. Look carefully, and you might see one buried in the sand.

Wow! Just imagine finding a shell as big as this one. You might, if you visit the island of Mauritius in the Indian Ocean. That's where this colorful giant triton shell was found.

If you find a spiral shell, such as a conch shell, try this: Hold the opening of the shell to your ear. What do you hear? The sound of the ocean!

Shells aren't the only wonderful things you can find at the beach. Down near the water, you might see a crab scuttling over the sand. In shallow tide pools, you may see snails and other live animals. Their shells

Maybe you'll spot a horseshoe crab at the beach. These odd sea creatures have been around since the days of the dinosaurs. That's a long time!

THE SNAIL

The snail he lives in his hard round house,
In the sand, under the sea:
Says he, "I have but a single room;
But it's large enough for me."

The snail in his little house does dwell
All the week from end to end,
You're at home, Mister Snail;
that's all very well,
But you never receive a friend!

protect their soft, squishy bodies. When a snail is scared, it pulls its body inside its shell. "Go away!" it seems to say. "There's nobody here!"

When you get your shells home, rinse them well. Let them dry, and keep them in a box. They will always remind you of your walk on the beach.

I SPY

I spy red-and-white
sunglasses, a blue comb,
and a yellow truck.
What do YOU spy?

Snow White and the Seven Princes

One day, the Seven Dwarfs got a note from Snow White. "Listen, men!" Doc said. "The Princess is coming to key us, I mean *see* us!"

"It's about time," Grumpy grumbled. "I thought she had forgotten all about us—now that she's married to her prince!"

"And she's coming for dinner," laughed Happy.

"Great," said Doc. "But if we're going to have a visit from a princess, we must act like princes!"

"How?" Bashful asked, looking down shyly.

"Well, I'm going to do my vest, I mean my *best*, to speak like a prince," answered Doc.

Happy laughed. "I'll try not to laugh so much. I'm sure princes don't laugh all the time."

Sleepy stretched and yawned. "I'll try to stay awake," he said as he began to doze off.

Grumpy snorted. "He'll need a bell to keep him awake!"

Dopey ran to the closet and found a bell. He tied it around Sleepy's neck. When he pulled on the rope, the bell clanged and Sleepy woke up!

"Good work, Dopey!" Doc said. "Now, news hext, I mean, *who's next?*"

Sneezy answered. "I'll wear a nose mitten. Then I won't smell anything that will make me sneeze."

Dopey looked around. He found a wooden whistle and held it to his mouth. Soon he was whistling a cheery tune.

"And I'll try to talk more to the Princess," Bashful said very quietly and slowly.

"Humph!" Grumpy growled. "I'll be in charge of the most important things—hand-washing and flower-gathering. We'll have the cleanest hands and the best flowers at the table for dinner. And don't any of you try to sneak a dirty hand past me!"

"Okay, men," said Doc. "I hereby announce the start of the Program of Princely Behavior!"

Snow White arrived the very next day. But when she stepped out of her coach, she was surprised to see that all the dwarfs were dripping wet!

"Why, good evening, everyone," Snow White said. "How did you all get so wet?"

Doc was too nervous to talk. He was afraid he would mix up his words. Instead, Bashful explained in a loud voice, "Grumpy wanted to make sure that we all had clean hands. So he dunked each of us in the pond!" And Bashful kept talking and talking and talking.

"Why, Bashful," said Snow White, with a puzzled look. "You're not so bashful anymore."

Then Grumpy ran to the front door of the cottage and picked up two big bunches of flowers. "Wait till you come inside," he said sweetly. "I picked every single flower in the forest!"

"Yup, every single one," agreed a voice that Snow White didn't recognize.

"Sneezy? Is that you?" Snow White asked. She could barely see his face behind the large blue mitten on his nose.

"Yes, Princess," he answered. "And now not even all these flowers will make me sneeze!"

Then Snow White heard a bell. Sleepy smiled at her and started to doze. But as his head dropped, the bell clanged and he jumped awake.

Snow White started to say hello to Sleepy, but just then Dopey came up. He was whistling merrily. "Why, Dopey, what a lovely whistle. Did you carve it yourself?" asked Snow White.

"He sure did," Bashful told her. Sleepy's bell clanged again, and the dwarfs' shoes squished as they walked.

My, my, thought Snow White, it's so noisy here today. Sleepy's clanging, Dopey's whistling, and everyone's shoes squishing made it hard to talk.

"How nice, Dopey," Snow White shouted over the whistling, clanging, and squishing. Then she spotted Happy. "What's wrong, Happy?" she asked.

Happy brushed his tears away with his sleeve. It was so hard not to laugh that he had to think unhappy thoughts that made him cry. "Nothing, Princess," he sniffled.

"But you're always so happy," Snow White said.

Happy just sniffled louder. Soon his sniffles were drowned out by all the squishing, clanging, and whistling.

Snow White frowned and asked, "Where is Doc?"
Doc would know what was wrong with everybody.

Doc was still afraid he would get his words mixed
up. So he pushed Bashful forward to do the talking.
"Could I speak with you, Princess? How was your
ride through the forest? Where is the Prince today?"

Snow White couldn't believe her ears. Bashful was
asking questions! "Well," she sighed, "I guess we
should sit down. What did you make for dinner?"

Suddenly the squishing, clanging, whistling, and
sniffling stopped. The dwarfs looked at each other.

"Dake for minner?" Doc said before he could stop himself. "I mean *make for dinner!*" Bashful blushed. Happy laughed. Sleepy fell asleep. And Sneezy put a finger under his nose mitten.

"AAAHHH-CHOOO!!!" With one sneeze, Sneezy blew the mitten off his nose. "Sorry, men," he said sadly. "I guess I'll never be very princely after all."

"What do you mean, Sneezy?" asked Snow White. "Why have you all been acting so odd?"

"We wanted to be like princes for you," Doc answered. "Princes don't mix up their words. Or laugh too much. Or have dirty hands. Or act bashful. Or sneeze too loudly. Or sleep so much."

"Oh," said Snow White. "But don't you see? I like each of you for the special thing that makes you different. You are princes to me just the way you are!" And she gave each dwarf a big hug.

Sneezy ah-chooed again. Sleepy dozed and Doc chatted. Happy laughed and Grumpy grumped. Bashful smiled shyly and Dopey played a merry tune. And Snow White smiled and made a stew fit for seven princes—her best friends.

COME TO THE CIRCUS

Ladies and gentlemen! Kids of all ages! Step right up! Watch the trained elephants, the prancing horses, and the wild animals. Laugh at the clowns. Gasp at the amazing stilt walkers. Thrill to the daredevil high-wire artists. Come to the circus!

Everyone loves the circus. There's so much to see! Animals and acrobats, stunts and surprises—the circus has something for everyone. It's no wonder that one of the most famous circuses calls itself "The Greatest Show on Earth"!

A big parade starts the show. All the performers march around the arena, and the circus band plays. Of course, the stars of the parade are the elephants. Everyone wants to see these huge, wonderful animals. Circus performers ride them, and the elephants are trained to do lots of tricks.

All the circus performers— even the elephants— wear beautiful costumes. The costumes glow with bright colors and glitter with sequins and spangles. Everyone in the audience claps their hands.

ELEPHANTS

What's the best part of the circus? Many people would say the clowns! With their painted faces and funny costumes, clowns keep the audience chuckling.

Circus clowns never speak. They just do crazy stunts. They tumble into the arena between acts.

CLOWNS

They even romp while other acts are performing. They juggle. They chase each other and pretend to fight. They race around on unicycles. Clowns are always up to something!

Stilt walkers are amazing when they balance on their tall "legs." And aerialists are so daring! High above the ring, an aerialist dances on a wire. Luckily, there's a net below!

Animals of all kinds are circus stars. Dogs dance to music. Seals balance balls on their noses. Monkeys do acrobatic stunts. Sleek horses carry bareback riders. Elephants stand on their heads.

Wild-animal acts are a very exciting part of the show. Inside a cage, a trainer faces snarling lions and tigers. The trainer cracks a whip, and the fierce jungle beasts respond to his commands. Some brave wild-animal trainers have even ridden tigers!

ANIMAL ACTS

A Special Kind of Circus

What's this? Is it a monster with four heads and eight legs? No! The heads and legs belong to acrobats from a very unusual circus.

The *Cirque du Soleil* ("Circus of the Sun") is from Montreal, Canada. It isn't like any other circus. It has no animals. And the clowns don't wear white makeup on their faces or baggy pants.

Instead, most of the performers do amazing acrobatics to the beat of rock music. They leap. They balance. They twist their bodies into strange shapes. The show has fantastic sets and wild costumes. You'll love it!

Next time you hear that "the circus is coming to town," try to join the fun. Everyone in the family will find something to enjoy. It's a super show!

CHIP AND LITTLE CHEEP

It was a busy day at the castle. All the Enchanted Objects were hard at work, and Chip wanted to help.

In the kitchen, Mrs. Potts was putting whipped cream on a cake. "Let me help, Mama!" said Chip. But when he tried to stir the whipped cream, it splashed all over.

"Oh, dear, Chip," Mrs. Potts sighed as she wiped his face. "You're too little to help with the baking. Run along and find someone else to help."

60

Chip walked into the hallway. Cogsworth was standing on a ladder dusting a suit of armor.

"Let me help!" Chip said. He found a dustcloth and climbed up the ladder next to Cogsworth. But he rubbed the armor so hard that it began to shake. Then it began to tilt. And then the armor fell with a crash, knocking the ladder over. Down went Cogsworth and Chip, too!

The armor's helmet landed on top of Chip. He was very lucky he didn't get hurt.

"Dear, dear," Cogsworth said as he lifted the helmet off Chip. "You're too little for this job, Chip. Run along and find someone else to help." So Chip ran down the hall into the dining room.

Lumiere was lighting candles on the dining table.
"May I help?" Chip asked. But as he hopped across
the table, he knocked over the water pitcher. Water
splashed everywhere, putting out the candles.

"My, my," Lumiere said, shaking himself dry. "Run
along, Chip. You can't help me here."

Chip started to walk past the library. He saw Belle
carrying a big stack of books. Surely Belle would let
him help her! But as he rushed into the library, he
tripped on the rug and went flying through the air.

"Chip, watch out!" Belle cried. She dropped the
books and caught him in her hands.

"Oh, my, you gave me quite a scare!" Belle said. Books were scattered everywhere.

"I'm sorry. I wanted to help, but I just made you drop the books," Chip said sadly.

"Don't worry," Belle answered. "I can pick the books up. Anyway, they're too heavy for you to lift. Run along. I'm sure you'll find someone else to help."

But Chip didn't think so. He walked into the
garden. "Maybe I really *am* too little to help
anyone," he thought.

Just then, he heard a small peeping noise. A tiny
bird was lying on the ground, crying.

"What's the matter?" Chip asked. The bird opened
and closed its beak. "Maybe you're thirsty," Chip
said. He hurried away and brought back some
water. The little bird drank it all but then started
to cry again.

"I know. You're probably hungry!" Chip said. He looked around and found some seeds for the bird. The little bird ate all the seeds. But then he started to cry again.

"You look cold," Chip said. "I'll make you a warm nest of leaves." Chip started to pile leaves around the bird. But when he touched its wing, the little bird cried even louder.

Chip looked at the bird more carefully. "Oh, I see what's wrong. Your wing is hurt!" Chip said. "I'll go get Belle. She can help you."

But when Chip started to leave, the little bird began to cry louder than ever. "I guess you don't want me to leave you alone," Chip said. "Don't worry. I won't leave you. I'll carry you to the castle."

Chip carefully scooped the bird up. "Whew, you're bigger than I thought!" Chip gasped as he carried the bird into the castle.

Puffing and panting, Chip hurried past Cogsworth in the hall, past Lumiere in the dining room, and past Mrs. Potts in the kitchen. When they saw Chip with the bird, all the Enchanted Objects followed him into the library.

Belle knew just what to do. She bandaged the little bird's wing. Then she made it a soft nest in a corner of the library.

Chip looked at the little bird. "I wish I could help him get well," he said quietly.

"Why, Chip, you already did!" Belle said. "You gave him water and food and carried him inside. You were the biggest help of all!"

"Cheep! Cheep!" the little bird called to Chip.

"Listen!" Chip said. "I think he knows I helped him." Chip was proud of himself.

He stroked the little bird's feathers and said, "I'm going to take care of him until he's well. I'll name him Little Cheep. Chip and Little Cheep! We'll be best friends!"

Dogs are our pals. They love to be with people. And people love dogs. That makes dogs happy! A happy dog wags its tail and wiggles its body. Have you seen dogs that wag and wiggle? What other funny things do dogs do?

Dogs love chase games. And it's a lot of fun watching a dog chase a ball and other objects. You throw the ball. The dog runs to get it and brings it back as fast as he can. You throw the ball again. The dog brings it back again. Some dogs will play "fetch" for hours!

Best Friends

Fetch It!

Have you ever seen a dog sniffing the ground outside? Dogs are super sniffers. A dog can tell who walked by hours ago, just by smelling the ground.

Dogs are also great diggers. Some dogs like to dig holes and bury

Come Here, Rover

bones and other treats. But they can't always find their "buried treasure" when they want it later. They may make lots of holes in the ground looking for it!

Dogs bark and whine and make many funny noises. Some dogs howl when they hear music. *"Oo-woo-ooo"*—they're trying to sing along with you. And some dogs howl when they hear police sirens and fire engines.

Does your dog howl loudly when you and your family go out? He howls because he misses you. Dogs don't like to be alone. They want to be with their families—the people who love and care for them. So when a dog's family leaves, he howls to say, "Please come back!"

DOG TALK

Make your dog happy. Learn "dog talk."

"Let's play!"

This dog wants to play. He crouches down in front and raises his rear.

"I'm scared!"

This dog is frightened. He tucks his tail between his legs, and he holds his ears back.

"I'm the boss!"

This dog is acting tough. He stands stiffly and holds his tail high. If he shows his teeth, he's saying, "Watch out! I might bite!"

"You're the boss!"

This dog wants to show that he won't hurt you. He crouches low and holds his ears back.

"I'm the baby!"

When a dog *really* wants to give in, he acts like a puppy. He rolls on his back.

What does your dog do when you come home? He jumps and barks and wags and wiggles. He's VERY happy to see you. No wonder we love dogs!

75

What's the Scoop?

I Scream
You Scream
We All Scream
for Ice Cream!

Just about everyone in the whole world loves ice cream. Ice cream is cool. It's creamy. It's sweet. It's dreamy!

76

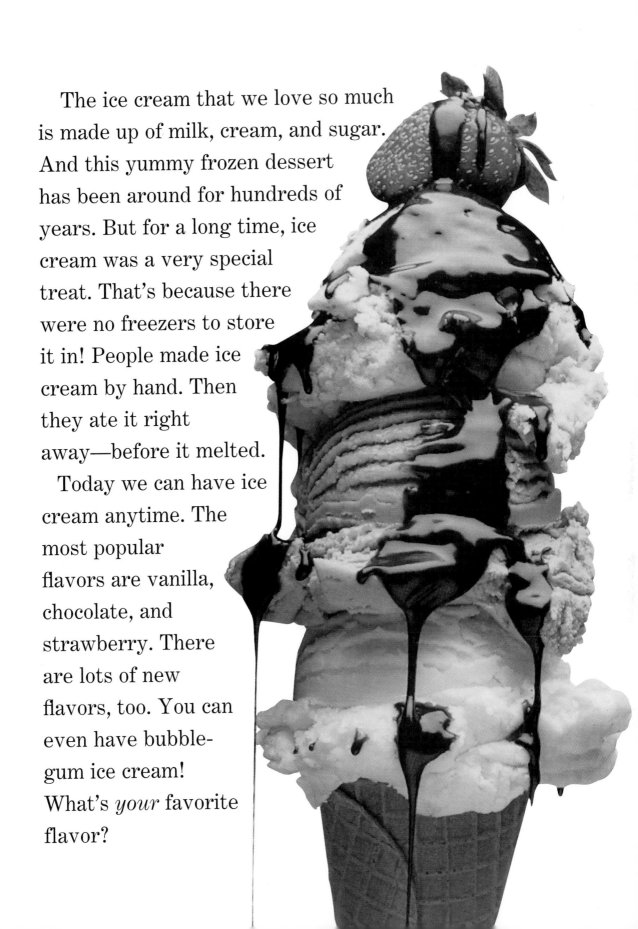

The ice cream that we love so much is made up of milk, cream, and sugar. And this yummy frozen dessert has been around for hundreds of years. But for a long time, ice cream was a very special treat. That's because there were no freezers to store it in! People made ice cream by hand. Then they ate it right away—before it melted.

Today we can have ice cream anytime. The most popular flavors are vanilla, chocolate, and strawberry. There are lots of new flavors, too. You can even have bubble-gum ice cream! What's *your* favorite flavor?

The Magic Coin

Pinocchio the puppet was looking out the window of his father's wood-carving shop. The wishing star twinkled brightly in the sky. Soon Geppetto would come home, and all the wonderful clocks in the shop would show that it was seven o'clock.

Pinocchio sighed.

"What's the matter, Pinoke?" asked his friend Jiminy Cricket.

"Oh," said Pinocchio, "I'm sad because Geppetto has made so many clocks and not one of them is mine. Not even the soldier clock, my favorite one."

"Why don't you just ask Geppetto to give it to you?" suggested Jiminy. "I'm sure he would."

Pinocchio looked up at the wishing star. "I wish he would," he sighed.

As Pinocchio and Jiminy watched the star, it began to grow bigger and brighter. Soon the shop was filled with a blue light, and a beautiful lady dressed in blue appeared.

"It's the Blue Fairy!" gasped Jiminy.

The fairy bent over and gently touched
Pinocchio's hand with her magic wand. Then she
spoke. "I heard your wish, Pinocchio, and I'm going
to grant it. Look in your hand."

Pinocchio opened his hand and saw a gold coin. It
twinkled in the blue light.

"That's a magic coin," explained the fairy. "It will
grant you five wishes. You may use them all, or
give some of them to someone else. But be careful
what you wish, Pinocchio. Good wishes are hard to
make."

"Oh, I won't have any trouble," said Pinocchio.

"Just listen to Jiminy," the fairy advised. "He'll
help you." And then she disappeared.

80

Suddenly all the clocks
began to tell the hour.
Pinocchio looked at his
favorite clock, which was
shaped like a castle. A
little drawbridge came
down, and out marched a
group of toy soldiers.
They raised tiny horns,
tooted seven times, and marched back into the
castle as the drawbridge closed behind them.

Pinocchio couldn't believe his good fortune. He
shut his eyes tightly and said: "My first wish is to
have the soldier clock as my very own!"

At that moment, Geppetto came in the door and gave his son a hug. "Pinocchio," he said, "you have been very good lately, and I want to reward you. You may have my soldier clock."

Pinocchio looked at Jiminy. "My first wish came true!" he whispered.

That night, as Pinocchio was getting ready for bed, he told Jiminy about his second wish. "I'm going to wish for a lot of money. Then I can buy a sled, and a pair of skates, and a pony."

"Be careful about wishing for *things*," warned Jiminy. "Things won't make you happy."

The next morning Geppetto went out and left Pinocchio in charge of the shop. The little puppet was sweeping the floor when a customer came in. He went straight to Pinocchio's soldier clock. "I must have this clock," he said.

"I'm sorry," said Pinocchio. "It isn't for sale."

"I'll pay you twice the price," said the man.

That was really a lot of money. But the soldier clock was Pinocchio's favorite, and Geppetto had given it to him.

"I'm sorry, sir," said Pinocchio firmly. "It's my very own clock. And it's not for sale."

"I'll give you five times the price," the man said. "I must have it!"

That was just too tempting for Pinocchio. All that money would buy the sled, and the skates, and a pony, too.

"Sold," said Pinocchio sadly.

The man gave Pinocchio the money and left—happily carrying the puppet's favorite clock.

When Geppetto came home, Pinocchio told him what had happened. "I'm sure going to miss the clock, Father."

"I'll miss it, too," sighed Geppetto.

"I wish I had it back!" said Pinocchio. Then he realized he had just made his third wish. At that very moment, the man who had bought Pinocchio's clock came into the shop.

"I bought this clock today," the man said to Geppetto. "But when I got home, it wouldn't run."

"Oh, that's no problem. We will be happy to give you your money back," answered Geppetto.

When the man had gone, Geppetto sat down at his
workbench to fix the soldier clock.

Pinocchio went quietly off to his room. He sat
down on the bed, and Jiminy hopped up beside him.

"Gosh, Jiminy," said Pinocchio. "Wishing didn't
turn out the way I thought it would. First I had the
clock I always wanted. Then I didn't have the clock,
but I had a lot of money. Now I have no money, but
I do have a broken clock. And I've already used up
three wishes!"

Pinocchio took the magic coin out of his pocket and walked over to the window.

"What are you going to do?" asked Jiminy.

"I'm afraid to make any more wishes," Pinocchio

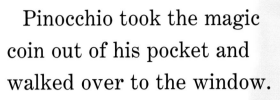

answered. Then he tossed the coin out the window. It landed on the street below.

"I just wish my clock weren't broken," Pinocchio said to Jiminy as he sat back down on his bed.

87

Just then Geppetto called up the stairs to his son. "Pinocchio, good news. Your favorite clock is working again!"

Pinocchio and Jiminy raced down the stairs. They got to the workshop just in time to watch the toy

soldiers march out of the clock and toot their horns four times, for four o'clock.

Jiminy smiled. Pinocchio's fourth wish had come true, just as the Blue Fairy had promised. But what would become of the fifth wish?

Neither Jiminy nor Pinocchio nor Geppetto saw the poor beggar woman who picked up the coin from the street.

"Oh, thank goodness!" she said. "I was wishing I could buy a warm coat for the winter. Now I can!" She didn't know that the coin she was holding was a wishing coin. She just knew that her wish, which was the fifth the coin could grant, had indeed come true.

PARTY POPPERS

Pooh has come up with some terrific party favors. You can make them, too. These colorful party poppers are just hollow cardboard tubes stuffed with goodies.

What you need:

- bathroom-tissue tubes
- printed wrapping papers
- different-colored tissue paper
- lollipops and other candy
- scissors
- white glue
- newspaper to work on

1. Cut out a circle from a piece of wrapping paper and glue it over the bottom hole of the cardboard tube. Then glue a strip of paper around the tube itself.

2. Fill the tube with lollipops and other candy.

3. Stuff some tissue paper into the tube. Let the ends of the paper stick out.

4. Tell your party friends to "pop" the tissue paper out of the tubes—and then eat all the goodies!

UNDERWATER SURPRISES

In many parts of the ocean, there are underwater kingdoms that are home to a rainbow world of animals and plants.

One such animal is the **starfish**. It got its name because it looks just like a five-pointed star. Most starfish have five arms. They also have five eyes—one on the tip of each arm!

A **sea anemone** may look like an underwater flower. But it's really an animal in disguise. Sea anemones spend their entire lives attached to rocks. And they live together in groups. Their petal-like tentacles are poisonous and can sting small fish.

Only **clownfish** are friends with sea anemones. Clownfish have a special coating on their skin, so anemones won't sting them. In fact, clownfish hide in the anemones' tentacles for protection against bigger fish.

The **mandarin fish** is one of the most colorful fish of the sea. Its bright colors help protect it. The colors warn enemies that the mandarin fish is smelly and bad-tasting.

Sponges come in many shapes and colors. They are unusual underwater creatures. They have no hearts, lungs, brains, sense organs, or nerves.

Corals are tiny sea animals. The coral's skeleton is made of limestone, and it grows outside its body! There are many different kinds of corals. The one shown here is called a mushroom coral. Do you know why?

The **pipefish** is often called a "dragon of the deep." Pipefish can be found hidden among rocks and seaweed. Their dazzling patterns help them blend into their surroundings and hide from enemies.

I LOVE TO SING!

There's nothing quite as wonderful in all the world as song.
Especially when I can get my friends to sing along.
But even when I'm all alone a song is company.
I sing of places far away that I can't wait to see.

I sing about my dreams and know
    that they'll come true someday.
And when the doubts and fears creep in,
    a song shoos them away.
Sometimes I find it hard to say
    the thoughts inside my head,
But then I think of music,
    and I sing my thoughts instead.

Sometimes I feel like I'll just burst,
    and I run off to hide,
'Cause no one seems to understand
    the way I feel inside.
But when I sing, my spirits lift.
    It never takes that long
Because there's something magical
    inside of every song!